Woman
Manifested

A Poetic Tale
By Lashuntrice

ISBN: 978-0692632932

DEDICATION

This book is dedicated to my imagination and anyone that has influenced it. If you've taught me how to be a friend, this is for you. If you've taught me pain, this is for you. If you've taught me about romance or lust this is for you. Whether you directly or indirectly taught me a lesson, you influenced my life so this is for you.

CONTENTS

Yesterday I Committed A Murder

Yesterday, I committed a murder, risked receiving twenty to life, all for a glimpse of excitement.

Wanted to see what it was like to live the Barbie lifestyle, throw on my pretty wig, ride out reckless and wild.

But no Ken for me.

Instead, seduce the Wayne's, Diddy's and then kick them to the curve for my own television show.

After all, pussy rules the world.

So I'd use my sex and have all the guys on TV screaming, "THAT'S A MILLION DOLLAR GIRL!"

Have my motto be "I'm so bad, I'm so hood, I'm the girl yo' man wish he could."

Work my way to the top using the road that many girls are willing to travel, then jump just to see what it feels like to fall.

But the fall wouldn't happen because someone would catch me, put a microphone in my hand, and stick me in front of an audience to reveal the secrets to success.

I wouldn't be a success.

More like a hot mess, but hot mess sells.

Thinking of the entertainment industry as I talk, I would tell them to kill their goals of being doctors, lawyers, and counselors and instead go for the next female rapper or reality star or pretty girl like me.

Money over everything would be so embedded on me that people would have no choice but to call me the baddest bitch, worship every ground that I walk on, and try to imitate my style.

They wouldn't be able to copy me though, cause I'd be so off the wall I'd have Oprah in awe.

I'd be so praised that committing that murder would be more than worth it; killing the innocent, scared little girl would pay off; killing the boring, monotonous, tiresome, always stuck in the same routine girl would be the best thing in the world.

Yesterday, I committed that murder, decided I wouldn't do twenty to life cause pretty girls aren't fit for prison. Now as I prepare to blend in the with crowd, but make enough noise to still stand out, the dream doesn't seem so far away.

This was written during one of my most stressful times. I was getting ready to graduate college and I had absolutely nothing planned for my future. I had no job lined up, no idea of how my bills would get paid once my parents officially cut me off, or if they would cut me off, and no idea where my talents fit. What I did have was a huge imagination, images of a whole bunch of other people's lives flowing through my mind, and a fairly new blog, which is now www.searchingformystar.com. I was absolutely lost when it came to where my life was going, but I knew better days were eventually going to come.

Introduction

For a moment she sounded strong again.

She laughed loudly as the memories of being in a relationship flowed back into her mind, the times of feeling butterflies deep down for her man, the moments of him sweeping her off her feet with the sweetest of surprises, the times of being comfortable just from the sight of him, and the moments she'd rather be alone.

As she questioned me about the man I allowed her to think I have she smiled and got lost in her own thoughts. She asked if I had spoken to him since I had been in town and I replied with a no. Then she started talking about how both he and I were avoiding each other for those several days. I wanted her to be happy, so I didn't spoil that moment for my great grandmother.

It was the summer of 2015 and I was seeing my great grandmother for the first time in five years. So much has changed. She is no longer the vibrant woman I remember growing up. She's no longer the active woman from a couple of years ago. Instead my great grandmother is frail. Although she sometimes talks as though she's still independent, she cannot stand up on her own. She needs all the help that she can get.

I watched her attempt to stand up on her own when she needed to go to the restroom. She leaned against her walker as she was sitting and tried to lift herself up. Her eyes watered and I started to get up and help her. At the same time I got the attention of my mom because I knew I wasn't strong enough to help her.

Just as quickly as my great granny is talking and full of life, she'll also drift to another world. She can barely remember who anyone is at times. While I didn't witness it, my mom says she talks to herself and the dead often. There are nights where she struggles to sleep and wants to be moved from her bed to the living room. It wears everyone else out, but they oblige. She is suffering from dementia. You may wonder why she isn't in a nursing home and the answer is simple. My great grandma is spoiled.

Her life started in 1928. There are stories she's told that I'm struggling to hold onto. I want to remember waking up in the mornings as a kid and drinking coffee with her. We were the only ones indulging in the delicious coffee, but we didn't need any other company. After moving to Houston at the age of 6, for years I'd only drink coffee when I went back to Plant City to visit her and my grandma.

It's a blessing that my great grandmother has made it to 88 years old. She's had a long prosperous life. She was married twice. My great grandmother has experienced the greatest moments of corporate America and the most tiring moments of being apart of corporate America too; even if her version of corporate America hasn't looked like mines. She's experienced everything. She's been able to see her children (4 of them) have children, her grandchildren have children, and even some of her great grandchildren have children of their own.

I wish I could give more information about her. However, if you search through the Internet and search through public record you'll find the basics of her life so far. That's her whole name, her date of birth, some of her family members, and where she currently resides. This reminds me that I haven't asked enough questions or maybe even asked the right questions in these 29 years of life. While she and others in my family have been good at collecting pictures, they don't have good documentation of who all is in the pictures or written documents on their own lives.

I can't give you a book on the life of my great grandmother or even my grandmother. I'm not sure if my mom would want me to document her every move for money making purposes, but what I can do is open up to you about my own experiences. I can give you a glimpse of how I've felt at various moments. I'm a storyteller so I can give you moments in stories.

I was once a child imagining the joys of adulthood. I couldn't wait to get my period until the day I finally got my period. I couldn't wait to say the word boyfriend and be able to refer to that boyfriend as mines. I couldn't wait to get that education so I could finally be living the lifestyle that college degrees promise. I couldn't wait to finally be independent and spend my money the way I prefer to. Now I am a woman and more confused than ever. My life revolves around balancing responsibilities, fun, and not going emotionally crazy from failed attempts at love. Hello, I'm Lashuntrice Chevelle Bradley and this is my manifestation.

The following is not a biography. I do not know how to give you a detailed account of every experience that has ever changed me. I do, however, know how to put experiences in a creative format. The following is my life creatively written through poetry. The poetry starts doing my college years and end in 2015. As you read, remember I'm an artist and I'm sensitive about my shit.

Pretty Bird

Pretty bird, pretty bird, are you ready for me to tear you apart?

I'm taking your life and examining it from here to afar.

What is your success record, what you have accomplished?

With your sweet personality, good grades, grades will only get you so far.

You're in the real world now, where no one likes you anymore.

If you've had enemies before, they'll increase like you've never imagined.

If you thought you had lots of friends, just watch the numbers dwindle.

Pretty bird, I see you're afraid of struggle.

Been on your own for a little bit...bills, bills, bills .

Now you see why Destiny's Child wanted a man to pay them.

They just keep coming and coming, forcing you to hustle harder.

Working harder while the numbers on the check don't seem to change.

Working harder, is your sanity still the same?

Are you enjoying life, living out your travel dreams, crossing a few places off the list?

Is that huge bed comfortable, because you'll be spending a lot of time sleeping alone?

Are you eating well, enjoying only the finest of delicious food?

Or has reality hit, over the years you've been fed some crazy shit.

How fun will come later and you'll be able to afford everything you want.

But now I've gotten you stuck right where I wanted you.

In the never ending cycle where hustle is the mentality and freedom is only a part of your imagination.

But pretty bird do not give up on me. You make a pretty slave in this cold world.

I was looking for a change of scenery. If not a new city, I could settle for a brand new job. I'm a girl with a creative imagination and a Bachelors degree to my name. I felt like someone should want me and want to pay me enough to really thrive in this world. However, finding a new job isn't easy when the new jobs all seem to creep toward minimum wage salaries. I'm a woman that never plans to move back in with my parents. The search was tough, but a job finally reached back out.

The job was similar to what I was already doing, but the vibe just didn't feel right the moment I stepped into the office for the interview. I was sent to a waiting room that felt like I was waiting for a doctor's appointment.

It was cold and super quiet. This may not make sense, but something about pure silence creeps me out. Others were in the room eating and sitting in their own corners. The waiting room also served as the break room for the co-workers so it gave me a glimpse of what kind of people I would be working with if I had chosen that career path. The room overlooked a street corner with lots of cars passing by. I felt like I was trapped in a cage as I watched others enjoying their cool adventurous lives. No one else seemed to be bothered by this.

I haven't been on another interview since then. I've barely submitted my resume anywhere. While sending out that resume sparks some excitement for new opportunities, getting rejection letters really hurts my self-esteem.

A Degree in BS

The crowd screams

The cameras flash

The questions get asked

"How did you do it?"

They want to know,

"How are you so successful?"

And I reply

I got a BS degree

And they ask

"What does BS stand for?"

Bull Shit...

See I woke up happy...Thought I had all I needed: education, degrees, the "white girl" grammar, the "almost" perfect body, the friendly attitude, the willing to do whatever it takes to achieve my dreams mood...Because someone once said, "Do what you have to do in order to do what you want to do" and after years of struggling to obtain something I thought I needed: hope, accomplishing goals, handing over my soul for a little bit of talent, I'm chasing after minimum wage jobs, living in the parents' house, and crying my eyes out because as good as this BS degree is it's never good enough. Some think my bullshit is too much for them... "That's a mean one, fast talker, too educated for her own good," while others say I can't spit enough Bull Shit for them. "Not good enough, lacking in Bull Shit skills, needs more experience in this Bull Shit world." But what keeps me going is those that praise my Bull Shit knowledge....

I hear their voices cheering me on

"How are you managing?"

They ask

"You see my Bullshit degree

I worked hard for this

So I'm putting these skills to work.

After all I didn't go through all this Bull Shit for nothing"

A harsh lesson in life that we are possibly never prepared for is the loss of friendships. Everyone has the same complaint when friends turn into strangers. We go from telling each other our darkest secrets to getting voicemails. We go from calling each other back to eventually ignoring phone calls on purpose. We go from seeing each other in the streets to social media being our only way of knowing that the people we used to be cool with are still alive. It becomes so bad that while we're connected on social media, we don't interact. I've had my own share of issues with friendships.

The first big issue with a friendship that I can remember was during my sophomore year of high school. It was with a girl who I'd met two years earlier in the 8th grade. At the time I switched from one school to another that was right down the road, but I lost contact with everyone I'd considered myself close to.

At this new school this girl was one of the first people I found myself having something in common with. What we had in common most was creative writing. Like me, she loved fiction. That one quality appealed to me so much I wasted no time calling her my best friend.

During our friendship we created some fiction stories together and we hung out when we weren't in school. In my freshman year of high school my dad purchased Bow Wow/ B2K concert tickets and she was the only one I could think of to invite.

After that our friendship started to fall apart. She started being mean to me. She was looking for reasons to push me away, but I was blinded by my own generosity. I usually brushed little problems off easily, so as soon as we'd have disagreements I would move on to happier thoughts. However, what I didn't realize was she wasn't moving on. It took a teacher to let me know that this girl was not the friend that I thought she was.

It started with a letter that she gave to this particular teacher. In it she discussed people she had issues with and how she wished they were dead. I was one of those people on the list. It confused me and scared me a little. I couldn't see why someone would want to hurt me or wish I were no longer living. Both the teacher and my mom suggested I separate myself from her. What I really wanted to do was get away from that small ass school. My mother had the power to actually put me in a new school because she was a teacher in the school district, but she didn't. Maybe I didn't push the problem enough.

I tried separating myself after that, but the situation became worse. She harassed me when she would see me around just because I didn't want to be around her anymore. She would come up to me trying to talk and get mad when I would tell her to leave me alone. She still had my number and had friends, so she persuaded them to call my number and harass me. Either they didn't think of it as harassment or they thought of me as that bad of a person, because they listened to her, picked up the phone and said mean things to me. My mother just wanted them to stop calling her house, but I didn't know how to make it end. I just wanted to hide.

The situation was bad on me mentally. I didn't want to ever refer to anyone else as a best friend anymore. The words best friend equated to enemy. The words held a level of hate and helplessness. I also didn't believe there was anyone that would protect me or stand up for me since no one did in that situation. Instead they turned against me.

By college I wanted to change my ways of thinking. I wanted to trust again. I wanted to have a group of girls that I could tell my deepest secrets and we could grow old together reminiscing on good times. Remember that television show *Girlfriends*? I wanted the friendships I saw others having and I wanted the bond those women created on that show. However, a couple weeks into my freshman year of college a girl that I'd just met accused me of being a bad friend. Her reasoning was that I wasn't hanging with her enough. The other girls who I lived in the same dorm with and had started hanging with took her side. They didn't act as if they wanted me around either. When we weren't in the dorms, they weren't inviting me to hang out with them or trying to find out where I was. I had flashbacks of the previous horrible experience, so I embraced being that bad friend and did not chase after them.

I didn't really want to be thought of as a bad friend though. I wanted to be around people that trusted me and cared about me as much as I cared about them. I wanted to care about my friends and not have my guard up. How could that become possible if I felt like everyone was looking for something to be wrong with me? Since the cost of counseling services were built in with college tuition, I spoke with a counselor about my issues. I went to two sessions and came to the conclusion that I'm not the problem.

I'm not bitter and I don't feel alone anymore. There are a couple of people I do consider really good friends, but for the most part I stay to myself. I wish I could explain why people have disliked me or why my phone isn't constantly ringing with invites to places. What I have learned is how to let people become strangers in the past. I've learned to stop chasing ghosts. The next poem is about those that I no longer communicate with.

Hotline Bling

I used to call you on my cellular device.

I wanted some friends, a couple of people I could depend on.

We could share stories of how our days went.

The good times, the crazy events, anything we missed.

And best of all we could create memories.

After all, once we'd become friends we would also be known as a clique.

Inseparable is how they'd see us.

Because no matter how close together or how far apart,

The goal was to always remain friends.

Remember how we made plans to be in each other's weddings.

And we'd be the aunties of each other's kids.

But friendships do fall apart.

You weren't one of those meant to be in my inner circle.

So numbers did get lost or purposely deleted.

What happened with us?

I look through my texts and you're not there.

And in pictures you disappeared years ago.

And every now and then when someone asks about you,

I don't know what to say.

My only reference is social media.

For some reason we still follow each other's online lives.

So do I lie to them and say you're doing fine?

Yesterday's Facebook post showed you smiling.

Or do I tell the truth?

I don't really care.

They same way you haven't spoken to me in years,

I stopped caring about you.

A couple of celebrity women are the representation of beauty for us all. If you look like Jennifer Lopez, you're beautiful. If you look like Beyonce, you're one of the most admired women in the world. If you look like Kim Kardashian you're guaranteed success and financial wealth for the rest of your life. If you're on a reality television show, being ratchet keeps money flowing through your bank account and the rest of us admire you for it. We even take advice from you.

Three of my favorite celebrities to look up to are Beyonce, Brandy, and Jill Scott. The following story was written as an ode to them.

Ghetto Girl

(She's art imitating reality.)

Once upon a time in a faraway castle there lived a...

Ghetto Girl

The day she was born she came out loud

Cries that disturbed the whole hospital

Tantrums that commanded everyone's attention

And the hair on her head was too much for anyone to handle

It was thick jet black with little sprinkles of red

Her pretty demeanor was cool

But her expensive taste was too much for her parents

They already had her in name brand clothes

Gucci, J. Lo, and anything designed by Kimora Lee

If they kept spending like that they'd go broke

So an evil nurse kidnapped her

Thought if she locked her away the world would be much safer

No one would know about big and colorful weaves

Freakum dresses, or even high-heeled sneakers

Blue, purple, and yellow nail polish wouldn't be popular

And it stayed like that for a while

But one day some man was bored

He was tired of dating women with straight hair

You know bone straight and wrapped at night to keep the style

And with a perm no girl can successfully achieve Shirley Temple curls

Plus, he was tired of girls with no goals other than to get married

He wanted a woman with real dreams

Such as opening up her own hair salon

Or becoming the next video vixen

The kind of woman that could rap as good as a man

Or sing so good he'd enjoy her voice in his dreams

Or create fiction the whole world would read

Or at least a big booty girl for him to make his wife

So he decided to search for excitement

That's why God says man finds his wife

And one day he found himself in the woods

When he passed by the castle

Looked up

And saw the most beautiful woman in the world

She was leaning out the window

"Hello" he said

"What it do" she responded back

He was amazed by her phrase

But failed to realize she had never even stepped foot in an elementary school

"What it is," she said after he failed to respond back quickly enough

"Let your colorful hair down. I want to see you."

"Ooh, no. Not my braids. I'll come open the door for you."

As she opened the door he fell in love

Big breasts stuffed in a shirt that showed off her flat stomach

And a fat ass that sat up in really short shorts

"On the other hand"

He said

"Coming into your house wouldn't be right"

"Let's go out and have some fun"

And she responded

"Do you have some money?"

He smiled,

 Took her out

And allowed her to change the world

Now every man wants a ghetto girl

And every girl wants to be her

She was a white girl on a campus full of black people. (*Let's call her Sharon, but that's not her real name.*) As awkward as Sharon's surroundings might have been for her, something even more awkward happened. She fell in love with a man that was already taken. This man had a girlfriend that he was publicly showing off, but he was sneaking around with Sharon in his free time. She needed someone to talk about her feelings with and for some reason she told me.

Sharon and I weren't friends. We entered college at the same time, had at least one class together, and knew each other well enough to speak in public. I was shocked Sharon would tell me about her situation since it was so sensitive but I was interested in hearing it. Afterward I asked her if I could turn what she was telling me into a poem. She was okay with it.

That is where *The Other Woman* comes in. I feel like this poem set me up for failure in some future relationships with men. Maybe they read it and thought I was okay with infidelity. Maybe a few men read it and spread rumors to make it harder for my love life. Maybe my imagination is just running wild, but at the time of writing this I'm still single and getting into a relationship becomes more difficult as time passes.

The Other Woman

Falling in too deep

But still trying to keep my head above water

However, he's making it hard

Cause I'm still feeling the pleasure from last night

How he kept kissing me softly

Wherever his lips were

They felt good

He started on my neck

Sucking until he gave me a hickey

Then slowly he started working his way down my body

Planting soft kisses on my breasts

And then trailing his lips down further

He stopped at my belly button

And kissed

And kissed

Until my body reacted

Then he was ready to go down further

And I was nervous

But at the same time excited

We had done this many times

But still I played it like it was my first

Let him help me remove my pants

And take my panties off

And when I was naked he dived in

Was ready to taste my juices

And taste is what he did

He licked, tasted, sucked, and tasted some more

And I caressed his head

Rubbed and pressed on him harder

As I got wet and wetter

And when he was finished

He was ready to dive in further

And I was ready for him

To feel his hardness inside of me

And as he entered

I caught myself whispering

"I love you,

Never want you to leave me"

But today is a different day

And as I feel myself falling too deep

Starting to drown in

L-O-V-E

I catch myself

Remind myself

He's with her now

The other woman

She's chillin' with him

Laughing as they watch

For The Love of Ray J

Cooking his favorite meal

I don't even know what that is

She's doing his laundry

And cleaning his house

Voluntarily playing wife

While I'm stuck at home

Sittin' by the phone

Waiting for his text

That says he's ready for more

She doesn't know about me

And neither does his friends

See him and I were never supposed to happen

But one class assignment forced us to exchange numbers

And during one meeting

We were supposed to discuss the assignment

But talking lead to touching

And touching lead to kissing

And kissing lead to...

Fucking, which is now the depth of our relationship

And unfortunately I want more

Want to know his hopes and dreams

What makes him happy

And what makes him sad

How to stroke his ego

Without first stroking his

D-I-C-K

And most importantly

I want to switch places with her

Side Chick

This poem is dedicated to my monogamous innocence. I never thought I'd agree to being with men that already had a long list of sex partners. I also never thought I'd agree with trying to get to know a man that was already seeing multiple women at the same time, or even put myself in the position of being the side chick. But I have.

Is it bad that I've never made love

I've never felt it

But I'm here with you

You're talking real explicit

Saying "Drop the good girl act

You don't want to be a girlfriend

Just play the side chick

Tonight's the night

No more innocence

Step out the sneakers

And leave the pants at home

Step into a short dress

Make sure it's easy to slip off"

Is it bad that you're tempting

Your soft brown skin

And that cologne you wear

It makes me want to get closer

And especially when you haven't shaved

The stubble on your chin

I just want to feel it

And is it bad that the words you say

That you've never been with a girl like me before

And you really don't want to

But you just can't leave me alone

Although you're not a chaser

And there's another girl by your side

She's a ride or die chick

While I'm a every once in a while chick

I can't figure out how to ignore you

Is it bad that I question if love even exists because you make me give up all faith in love and relationships, give up the good girl lifestyle, no more wishing for monogamous commitment, just take whatever I can get, even if that means settling for being the side chick?

At this point you may wonder what causes a woman to value the attention of men more than friendships. It's really all part of the design. From fairytales to teen magazines, getting that love of a significant other has been taught. It's not my battle alone either. I've had a countless amount of friends that stopped hanging with me to be with their boyfriends. I just haven't been as lucky as them.

In my almost 30 years of life two men have referred to me as their girlfriend. Neither of them lasted long enough to be considered husband material.

The first one was really cool. I met him when I was hanging with a group of people in Phase III, on campus apartments at Florida A&M University. When we started talking it was an instant connection. Everyone abandoned us when they noticed and we talked alone for hours.

After that, we saw each other a couple of times and in one of those instances, he asked me to be his girlfriend. I said yes because I was attracted to him and it was a new experience for me.

During our relationship we spent time alone a couple of times, but we never did anything past talking. There was no kissing and no sex. For most of our relationship he did these crazy disappearing acts. He was majoring in architecture. It was really tough and he would he deal with it by cutting everyone off for a period of time. A combination of feeling ignored during that time and being around other cute guys caused me to end the relationship.

Actually, it wasn't just being around other cute men. When I met him, I had never been kissed before. Since he was supposed to be my boyfriend, he should have been my first kiss. However, since he wasn't around some other guy took that opportunity. That was when I officially knew the relationship wasn't working out. Years later we reconnected and I threw out the idea of trying again. He said he wasn't the type to give the same girls a second try.

Soon after that breakup, I lost my virginity, but not the way I wanted to. There was nothing special to it. I wanted to have sex around that time. I felt ready, but I didn't want it to be with this particular guy. I wasn't even attracted to him in a sexual or romantic way. One of my friends, who I no longer speak to, was attracted to him. However, I trusted him enough to go to a house party with him and his roommate.

That night we went to the party and had lots of fun. After the party he dropped his roommate off and told me that he would only take me home if he could spend the night. I agreed because I didn't want to sleep at his place. I can't remember how quickly he mentioned having sex, but he knew I was a virgin. Everyone around that time knew I was a virgin. I remember him asking and I initially said no, but then said yes. He was already way too close to me and touching on me. He had a condom on him, which was the best part of the experience. I just remember laying there not really moving the whole time. I also remember him mentioning that he didn't really believe I was a virgin to begin with once it was over. As we fell asleep he wanted to cuddle and I kept pushing him away from me until I was too sleepy to keep pushing his arm off.

I really wanted this guy to understand my feelings toward him, so I made some things clear. I told him not to tell anyone what happened and explained that we wouldn't be having sex again. We would see each other around a couple more times and then he just disappeared out of my life. I couldn't be totally mad at him for disappearing. He kept his promise about not telling anyone.

The second guy I dated came years later. He was someone I should have absolutely said no to. I didn't know him. I talked to him a little online, met him in person, and said okay when he asked me to be his girlfriend. That relationship is one that I sometimes don't even claim. It lasted a month and he broke up with me. When he did the break up, he claimed he wanted to keep me around for sex. That was not about to happen. I was done with him.

The rest of the men that have come in my life were just friends, friends with benefits, or someone else's friend that I just happened to be around. I don't have a lot of experience in the dating world. Some of the men that have expressed interest rejected me the moment I said I was a virgin. Some men rejected me because they weren't looking for a relationship and were polite enough not to waste my time. Some saw me as just a friend of a friend. Some of the men I consider friends have been restricted to phone conversations only because of distance.

I haven't met a man yet that was really trying to cater to my needs or one that put my feelings first. There are a couple of men I know that will feed my fantasies with words. A guy from my college days said he would marry me if I was an immigrant and it was my only way to stay in the U.S. Another one has said several times that he wants to take me out on a memorable date, but it hasn't happened. There is this guy on my Facebook friends list that will remind me every couple of months that he's waiting on me, but I'm not sure what he is waiting for. However, I haven't given up on real romance yet. That is what the next couple of poems are about.

Make You My Boyfriend

If you hold my hand, I'll make you my boyfriend. How long has it been? Two? Three? Four months since the last man? Maybe it's been a whole year. I'm lonely. All this running around; to the mall, the movies, and dates at nice restaurants all by myself. I've even tried to solve this problem in rooms with the lights down low, slow grinding with some stranger as Waka Flocka Flame yells "Bow Bow Bow," but so far no luck. The clubs are just not made for prince charming. Wait, where'd I meet you again?

If you kiss me, it means we have to take it to the next level. No longer are there needs for questions of forever. Let's have sex like college students. Take my clothes off right here in this living room. Not a shirt, nor a bra, or buttons should deter you. Let's pretend you don't have a bed. We'll have sex everywhere else instead. Leave carpet burns on my back. But wait, you can't have all the fun. Let me get on top, ride you, pleasure you so good that for weeks all you'll be able to think about is Lashuntrice. This is not a game.

If you talk dirty to me there's no telling how far we'd go. Treat me like the other woman and call me a heaux. Your little slut? That bad Bitch that you just wanna fuck? Yeah, I hear you. Keep talking. Put me in a daze, so days later people will still be asking why I'm smiling.

There comes a point where we as women want that significant other so bad we'll say and do anything. The loneliness becomes unbearable and just the sight of a couple together make us feel inferior. While knowing independence and loving oneself is good, no woman wants to be single forever. I do want the love of a significant other, but I've also learned getting that from a man isn't easy. There are the attractive men that don't even know I exist, the ones that see me as just a friend, and the ones that are already taken. That's where *Every Fuck I Can Feel* comes from. Sometimes I just want to take what I can get in the moment. I was in a club when this came story came to my mind.

Every Fuck I Can Feel

I'm giving him every fuck I can feel. In the middle of the night in the midst of a packed club as our eyes meet all I can think about is being satisfied. It's been a while.

From the first crush, which was also the first man that said "Not interested," I started building a wall. His rejection hurt me in a way that I could never describe. Not to my mom, not to my dad, and never to friends. I let the tears fall, but made sure only I could see them. I sucked the pain up and learned to hold it within. I wanted to believe in love, but knew hurt came with it too. So I tried to pursue it while also protecting my feelings. I wanted passion but also wanted to give 0 fucks.

So after the first guy fucked me and said he wasn't looking for commitment I said, "Fuck it."

Then a guy eased his way into my life through a class one of us was required to take; that college lust. To the outside world, he was innocent but in getting to know him I knew better. I was a little more guarded so things never really progressed. I wasn't giving him what he wanted, so eventually he would give up and disappear, but to protect my feelings all I could do was say, "Fuck it."

With every guy that came into my life, made a trail of pain, and then I convinced myself that I didn't give a fuck until one day I was left alone and lonely and craving the affection not giving a fuck had denied me.

So during this night in the middle of the club as he stared at me with those sexy brown eyes and pressed his body against mine so I could feel his hardness I decided to give him every fuck I could feel. We were already hidden by the crowd; VIP section that night. On a couch countless others had already been on, my legs wrapped around his waist, his pants sagging, my heart unprotected, and his penis unprotected, he fucked me and I responded with every emotion I had.

This night never really happened.

Dance for Me

Remember when Beyonce came out with that song *Dance for You*? Well, as seductive as it was all I could think about is how I wanted a man to pay attention to what I wanted.

Tonight you'll dance for me.

Figure out a way to cater to my needs

Prepare a nice candle lit dinner

Treat me to my favorite food

I heard you want to show me

How much of a gentleman you can be

$1 + 1 = 2$

So tonight you won't be one-deep

Instead we'll start a countdown

To the countless amount of times

Remind me why I'm your baby

I'll get spoiled off your loving words

Sweet, kind, sexy, loving, fine, caring

Beautiful is how you see me

Tonight you'll give me everything

No more lies

You weren't at your mama's house

No more empty promises

No tomorrow you will take me out

You'll respect my time

So by tomorrow you'll have me looking crazy in love

Telling my friends there's nothing out there for me

Getting ready to ring that alarm

At the thought of you with another girl

You're not the only one that's insecure

So tonight you'll dance with me

So by the end of the night

I'll know why we're meant to be

Until the end of time

Dim The Lights

This was written as my version of Future's *Turn On* the Lights. It was also my way of showing I have a jealous side and if a man is special enough I think about him long after we've ended.

Dim the lights cause you found me.

Keep them low

No need to look anymore

You ain't want the girl from the corner

She was too hood

Had another nigga's name tattooed on her

And she kept calling you her future baby daddy

But you ain't want baby mama drama

And you ain't want the woman on Wall Street

If money was the answer, her pockets ran deep

But you ain't a broke nigga

You got your cash right

You looking for a woman that ain't thirsty

But you can take around the world

So I came your way

I think it was yesterday

You saw me driving that Hyundai

Had dreams of hittin' this one day

Well tonight is the night

The lights won't go off

But we won't need 'em too bright

Dim the lights just enough

So as our cries of pleasure sound in the middle of the night

And you make me cum over and over again

Dim the lights

Make the moment special

Look into my eyes

Because maybe I'm not the one for you

Maybe in your heart you're still searching for her

So dim the lights

Cause one day when you meet her I'll wish it was me

And I'll let the world know that I'm jealous

Sabotaged Love

The love was sabotaged from the start

Me already struggling with a broken heart

You not really wanting to get involved

But the chemistry would not let us be apart

Flirting for weeks

No talking

Just eye contact giving away our physical needs

Our body gestures speaking volumes

But the day I spoke gave away my shallowness

It was easy to tell your brown skin I wanted

Your clothes I wanted off

Your sex appeal having me whispering

The mind games as you whispered back

Left that night inevitable

Wasting time with foreplay

R. Kelly, Keith Sweat, Ja Rule to set the mood

You start with a surprise kiss

Trying to be romantic like the movies

But we rush to get clothes off

No more postponing intercourse

No condoms

You always felt they were uncomfortable

No birth control

I lied when I said I was on the pill

That night we start off clumsy

As Sex Is On My Mind plays in the background

But then find a nice rhythm

As Miss Pretty Pussy plays softly

But as the sex gets better

The sounds in the room get noisier

Our two skin tones

Your light skin

My almond complexion

Blend into one

The music no longer matters

See it was sabotaged from the start

There was no first date

No flowers and candy to show your affection

No kind words to share our appreciation

It wasn't old school

No one did any chasing

But by the end of that night it didn't matter

Everything still felt just right

Freedom

One day I'll set you free

You're not happy I can tell

But I can't let go of this unhealthy obsession for you

Your big brown eyes

The smell of your cologne

The feel of your skin against mine

Your hugs and kisses

The moment where I can tell it's me you miss

Unlike other men you have a drive

Plan A, B, and C

And rejection doesn't hurt you

One day I'll set you free

But for now I'll stick by your side

You're not a doctor yet

Too long before being a lawyer is confirmed

There's no money in being a 21st century artist

And the industry keeps shutting down your rap style

As hard as I try I can't seem to really get to know you

My cooking isn't good enough

That's why I struggle with the idea of doing it for you

And my sexual appetite isn't compatible with yours

And I don't even live with you

But you feel trapped

You'll never admit it though

Never show emotion

But for as long as I hold on, you will too

Naked

This poem was written about a guy I was attracted to, but at the same time couldn't figure out why he was so difficult to get to know. It was also inspired by a song, *Naked*, by the singer Trevon "John Dough" Wilson.

The goal is to get him naked, strip him to the core, seduce his mind, and make some of his time become mines.

This is about more than the physical, getting lost in his brown eyes, or comfortably resting on his chest. Cuddle time can come later, and although sex is immediately on his mind, and I'm curious about his D-game we have to wait, get to know stuff about each other, like what's his favorite color, and his favorite food, does he snore when he sleeps, and what are his biggest dreams.

But even if I fall victim to his touch, one minute we're talking, the next we're naked, on the couch, or the backseat of his car, getting lost within each other, even though we barely know each other, I still can't help but be curious afterward about who he is and how can I explore him?

His Addiction

On a Sunday morning in the middle of church he finds himself thinking about it. As the pastor preaches about abstinence, pregnancy tests, fathers being absent from their children's lives, and how all the problems of the world can be solved by following the word of God, he can only daydream about it. It feels like it's been a while, but he really just got some last night.

It came from a pretty girl. She was young, short, and shaped like a Barbie. She had a natural hairstyle, but dressed like one of the women from a music video. People from around the way said she was smart and even had a college education, but he didn't care. He wasn't mentally attracted to her. It was her physical parts that called to him, a special part of her that enticed his thoughts from the moment he saw her. It was her pussy.

He dreamed of getting into it. He dreamed of getting her alone in any room and spreading her legs apart. Whether it was a nice comfortable bedroom or a dirty warehouse did not matter. If all it took was an empty classroom and testing out how sturdy a teacher's desk was with their bodies on top of it intertwined together, he would have done it in a heartbeat. He wanted her pussy. He had to have it. It was what made him happy. It was what lit up his life.

He was not always a feign for her pussy though. There was a time in his life where he did not know what he liked. Nothing made him happy. Not recess or going to the park. Videos games didn't entice him. Sports games were a bore. Hanging with friends was not even an option. Nothing his parents did changed his mood. They always told stories about how he came out of the womb with a frown on his face. It was as if he was contemplating his place in the world from the very beginning. Many people say he spent the first 15 years treading through life. Then one day he all of a sudden perked up and smiled.

That was the day he learned about pussy. The lesson came from a wise old man on a street corner. The old man was skinny, had on a long coat from the winter cold, and did a whole lot of smiling. He wanted to know what there was to smile about at a time where it was freezing, but people were still forced to continue boring activities outside of their house. The old man's answer was one simple word.

"Pussy."

For some reason even before he met the first girl that would let him get a special piece of her world he smiled. Something about the world pussy made him happy. So he planned out how he would get it. Well, actually he just planned to ask some random girl he always saw around. It wasn't hard either. She already liked him so she invited him over when her parents weren't home. She didn't want to come off too easy so she forced him to sit through a movie and then played some slow jams to set the mood. She felt it was right, so she gave him exactly what he wanted. Neither of them knew what they were doing, but that didn't matter. When he slid himself into her tight wetness he was in Heaven.

Then he learned that being into exercising, sports, and videos games attracted women in more, so he developed hobbies just to get more pussy. At the age of 20 some girl finally let him fulfill his fantasy of doing it against that wall. He wanted to see how the pussy felt under his total control. At 24 he met a flexible girl willing to try out many positions. At 25 he found out he was the father of a beautiful daughter. It scared him for a moment because he knew what the power of the pussy would make a man do. His daughter couldn't go through all that, but then his worries were put aside when his baby mama got back in shape and dragged him back into the bedroom for a memorable night of sex.

He was in love. It was not necessarily with her but what she possessed. He knew then that as long as he was able to get pussy there would never be a sad moment in his lifetime again. He was forever happy.

Breakfast Can Wait

There's a saying that food is the way to a man's heart, so this is the plan I've devised to get the man of my dreams to finally pay attention to me.

Breakfast can wait. No eggs, sausage, or pancakes. I need to know that I have your attention in a different way. Do you see what I have on? This extra long shirt, for you I'm wearing it as a dress. It was your advice. You said it would look nice, so I copied your style. You said you need your woman to look good, speak proper, and have no baby daddies on her trail. You said you don't like women from the hood, so I'm pretending I was raised in an upper class neighborhood. So do you like what you see? Do you like me?

Lunch will be pushed back a little longer. Hold the sandwich, the chicken wings can wait, and no sipping of wine in the mean time. I need to figure out your mind. Have you seen my face? This bright red lipstick is meant to hold your attention. I'm trying to make sure you hear the words that are coming out of my mouth. I've been docile, following your every command. I've listened. You've said you want a woman that respects you, a woman that listens, hears your hopes and dreams. I heard you when you said you wanted to be a rapper, even listened to you freestyle those lyrics, and then you changed it up, decided you'd be better off as an actor. That's where the real money is. Even if you don't have the talent, I've made the decision to support you till the end.

Dinner may never come. There are more important topics than food, like will you support me too? Even if I quit my job to paint beautiful pictures in the form of words. They say there's no money in the writing game. Or what if I run off and join the circus. I need you to follow me hand in hand. Don't act surprised when it happens. I'm crazy man, but that's what you like. You say you're not looking for the good girl to make your wife. She's boring. She's annoying. I can give you excitement; make your life just right.

Finally, my eyes are open. I think about you all night long. I just need to know that you think about me too.

Willy Wonka

I'm crazy

Call me Willy Wonka

Cause I want your chocolate body

White chocolate

Light chocolate

Sweet chocolate

Dark chocolate

Milk chocolate

Pure chocolate

Just you and me

Just me and you

Just the two of us

Imagine where we could be

Laid up somewhere in Jamaica

Getting our groove on

Or running wild through the city of love

Or even chilling in paradise

Imagine enjoying the beauty of Hawaii

While we explore each other's minds

You gotta learn your man while you earn your man

So I'll never get tired of you

Let's elope in Vegas

It's never too early to start a lifetime of romance

Why don't we fall in love?

Like that Amerie song

Come with me

Tomorrow's not guaranteed

Pieces

This poem was inspired by Tamar Braxton's song with the exact same title. Her song was so deep that I had just had to create m own version.

I deserve more than just a little part

I don't want nothing if I can't have it all

You just wanted sex

Thought you could turn me on

Told me ways that you could please my body

And stupid little me

I decided to play your game

Only late night meetings

No early morning phone calls

Get lost in the moment

Get caught in the pleasure

So I don't have to think of the pain

Emotional anguish that voids good sex

The loneliness that replaces the facts

You was in my bed

I let you see me at my most vulnerable state

I let your naked body combine with mine

I knew you weren't mine

You saying you missing me

I don't want to hear it

You're all about the physical

Nice breasts

Nice legs

Nice lips

You want to kiss them

But I don't want to think of you

Don't want your bird chest

You should hit the gym more

Don't want your lame lines

Every other guy used those too

You don't want to make a woman out of me

Only trying to see how slutty I can be

No caring of the beautiful family we could be

You only want physical pieces of me

Can't you see I'm hurting

It's gonna be hard for me

But I'm not gonna give you any more pieces of me

I had this conversation with a former classmate that I still keep in touch with about how becoming a mother was creeping heavily into my mind. The idea has embedded itself so much that I've picked a specific year to really start attempting to have that child. The only problem with the plan is that I'm single.

Once I finished talking the classmate passionately told me to not to rush anything. She said as Black women, we have to be better at becoming wives and not just baby mamas. She's a mother of three and married to their father. While I agree with her, I can't make any promises that me becoming a wife will come before me becoming a mother. I also can't make any promises that I'll be the best mother, so I wrote this poem to the child that might one day question my parenting ways because they have to live with my mistakes.

The following poem was inspired by Bassey Ikpi's poem *Apology to My Unborn*. It's also based off the myth that single mothers turn into terrible parents.

Apology to My Unborn Child

I thought I'd met the man of my dreams. I thought I was in love. On many occasions we talked, kissed, hugged, until finally it led to breath-taking passion. I was always one to back off before it was too late. I was always one to back off before my feelings became trapped, but before I could leave him his seed, you, was already growing inside of me. He had already confessed his love for me. He had already put his trust in me, so the best thing to do was stay with him and have you.

But in all honesty I wasn't ready and I blamed you for putting my life on hold. I blamed you for not achieving my goals and I'm sorry because you were just an infant, a small child filled with lots of innocence and at night when the tears came down your sweet little eyes and I should have picked you up and held you until they dried, I'm sorry I didn't. I was too busy waiting for someone to wipe away my own tears.

I'm sorry for focusing so much on myself. The money that I spent on the shopping trips and getting my hair and nails done should have went to you. You should have had more clothes, toys, and you should have felt loved. I should have hugged and kissed you every chance I got. I should have made sure to show you that I loved you with all my heart. Instead I backed off. I forgot to kiss you. I forgot to hug you. I forgot to tell you that I loved you. I don't know why. Maybe it was because you looked so much like your father and he had stopped caring about me.

Thing is I'd always dreamed of a having a kid. I dreamed of changing lots of diapers, missing lots of sleep, holding you and spoiling you so you'd never want to leave my side but I messed up. Before I could be a mother I forgot how.

I'm also sorry for leaving you fatherless. I didn't know how to handle his love. I didn't know how to take care of him, you, and me and still have peace. I didn't really know what he wanted from me. I'm sorry I had to watch you grow up into a bitter adult because you grew up thinking I didn't love you and you didn't understand how a mother could purposely neglect her child. I'm sorry for it all. I hope you can forgive me one day.

Sincerely,

The Mother You Needed

Strong Black Woman

For some reason when you're a single black woman with some accomplishments, enough money to take care of yourself, and some goals people assume you are this strong black woman. Or is that me? One day I was feeling emotionally drained and I started writing this strong black woman poem.

I don't want to be a strong black woman anymore

Being strong means to handle anything

Being blind to the hatred

Shedding no tears

Putting on a pretty girl mask

Having no fears

I don't want to be strong

After dealing with years of verbal abuse

Being told I'm not pretty enough

Somebody said she's better

Not having the perfect skin

Nor the perfect body

Being told nobody wants me

Because somebody thought it was funny

If being strong means to smile anyway

When love or lack thereof comes around

And it knocks me down

If being a strong woman means getting back up

And pretending like nothing ever happened

Someone else can have the title

I'm tired

Tired of trifling ass men

In the beginning, they act like gentleman

Throwing out nice compliments

Suggesting going on dates

But then they never make anything happen

And I'm tired of the daddies that forgot to comfort their daughters

He claimed he'd wipe her tears away when she was hurt

And keep the bad guys away with his overprotective interrogations

But after handling finances

And getting out of 12 hour work days

That daddy is nowhere to be found

And I'm tired of the mamas pushing their daughters to be strong black women

She's only two

Teach her how to cook and clean like her mama

And teach her how to look up to her daddy

Teach her about meeting her prince charming

Don't teach her how to be strong

How to pay all the bills on her own

So one night she'll find herself at the bar

She'll be flirting with some man

But the drinks will be on her

Cause even he's fallen into the myth of the strong black woman

He'll think she can handle it all on her own

He'll think that he'll have to do nothing to get her

He'll devise of plan to get her out of her dress

Or maybe he'll just lead her on and never actually call

But it'll be okay because she's a strong black woman

She can take rejection

She can handle pain

See don't teach her that

She'll never grow up to be what you want her to be

Instead she might turn into me

But I don't want to be that woman anymore

Someone else can have that title

I'm tired

A Moment of Freedom

There's a picture on my blog. In the picture I have on a red wig, pink lipstick, and blue eye-shadow. I'm not sure where I was going that day, but it definitely was not to work. This poem A Moment of Freedom is all about that picture.

Red hair, Don't care.

Tired of being the same old me

No more aiming to please

So today I put on my red wig

Those other girls black and blonde

They're not trying to stand out

"Blend in, Blend in"

They whisper for me to do the same

There's no success in change

But I'm tired of listening

Red wig

Bright blue eye shadow

Loud pink lipstick

There's a camera

I smile and say cheese

But they don't see me

In their eyes there is the same old girl

Stuck in the same quiet world

She has no real goals

No achievable dreams

When was the last time she smiled?

When was the last time she cried?

No emotions are found in her face

There's no home to call her own

No real potential because she never listens

But I have potential

It lies in my freedom

So I look in the mirror

First goes on the bright blue eye shadow

So when they look in my eyes

They'll see a brand new girl

then goes the pink lipstick

A color reserved for brave Bitches

Topped off with a noticeable red wig

All put together shows a new girl

New confident attitude

It was my choice and I liked it

New brave stature

If I can do this, I can do anything

But it's only a moment of freedom

By tomorrow it'll be different

In the real world I'll listen

I'll aim to blend in

And become invisible again.

Usually books about womanhood are based on successes. They're written to uplift little girls and teach them about possible problems they'll face as young women. The books are written to teach little girls how to avoid those problems or how to survive when faced with the issues. This wasn't meant to be that kind of book.

Woman Manifested first came to my mind when I heard Jill Scott's *Womanifesto*. I wanted to be inspired by her words and create from the energy she gave in that poem. Although her story is different than mine, I feel that I achieved that goal and hope you feel that way too.

I'm not perfect and I'm not afraid to admit it. I've been hurt and I've hurt others, but I survived. I'm a woman with good and bad memories. I'm a woman that knows how to cry through the pain, but smile through the good times. I'm a woman that knows how to keep living her life to the fullest. I'm a woman that loves herself for who she has become.

 I wish I could give you more, but this is really just the beginning of my love story. For more of my writing you can go to http://www.searchingformystar.com.